THIS IS A GLOOP.

# THIS IS ANOTHER GLOOP.

THIS IS A GLOOP TOO.

# What are Gloops?

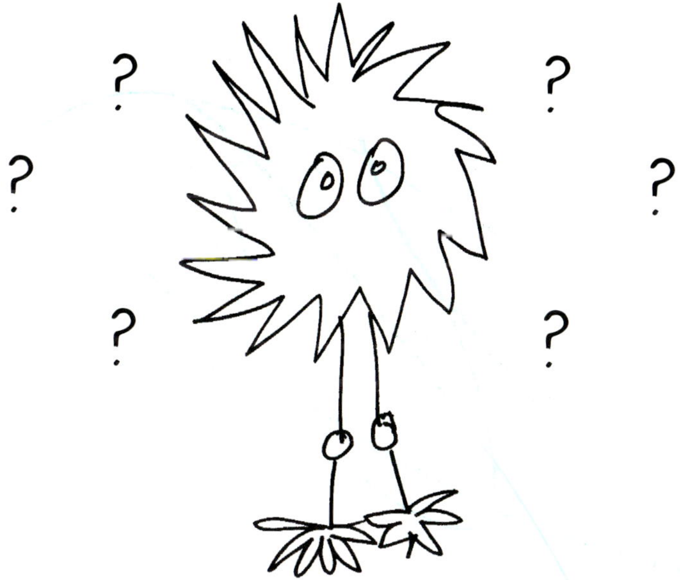

WELL GLOOPS ARE GLOOPS.

# AND THAT'S A GOOD THING.

BECAUSE IF THEY WERE
ELEPHANTS, WE WOULD BE
IN A LOT OF TROUBLE.

No one can really say what Gloops are, because no one has actually seen a Gloop alive.

GLOOPS RUN
VERY, VERY, VERY FAST.

THEY'VE NEVER STOPPED
LONG ENOUGH FOR
ANYONE TO SEE THEM.

I TELL YOU THIS
BECAUSE THEY ARE THERE.

SCIENTIFIC RESEARCH,
CONDUCTED UNDER
LABORATORY CONDITIONS,
HAVE GIVEN US TWO
INDICATORS ABOUT
THE PHYSICAL
CHARACTERISTICS
OF GLOOPS.

THROUGH CAREFUL EXAMINATION
OF GLOOP DROPPINGS
AND INVESTIGATING
HEREDITARY AND EVOLUTIONARY
ENVIRONMENTS, WE CAN MAKE
ASSUMPTIONS AS TO THEIR
SIZE, BODY STRUCTURE, AND
WHETHER OR NOT THEY LIKE
CORN FLAKES.

GLOOPS LEAVE EVIDENCE
OF THEIR EXISTENCE.

THERE ARE GLOOP DROPPINGS
ALL OVER THE PLACE.

You will be able to find dead Gloops under the bed, in the drawers, lint filters and in your pockets after they are washed.

BUT THE BIGGEST SINGLE INDICATOR THAT TELLS US WHAT GLOOPS LOOK LIKE IS WHEN YOU FIND DEAD GLOOPS IN THE DRYER FILTER.

HAVE YOU EVER BEEN
IN A ROOM ALONE AND
FEEL LIKE SOMEBODY
IS WATCHING YOU?

YOU TURN AROUND AND
NOTHING IS THERE!

THAT IS BECAUSE
GLOOPS RUN AND HIDE.

I TOLD YOU THAT
THEY ARE FAST.

THEY MOSTLY LIVE IN
RETURN AIR VENTS.

You may still feel that Gloops don't exist. Well, just take your finger and run over your desk after a few days of not cleaning or not dusting and you will pick up obvious samples of Gloop droppings.

"DON'T TELL ME THEY DON'T EXIST."

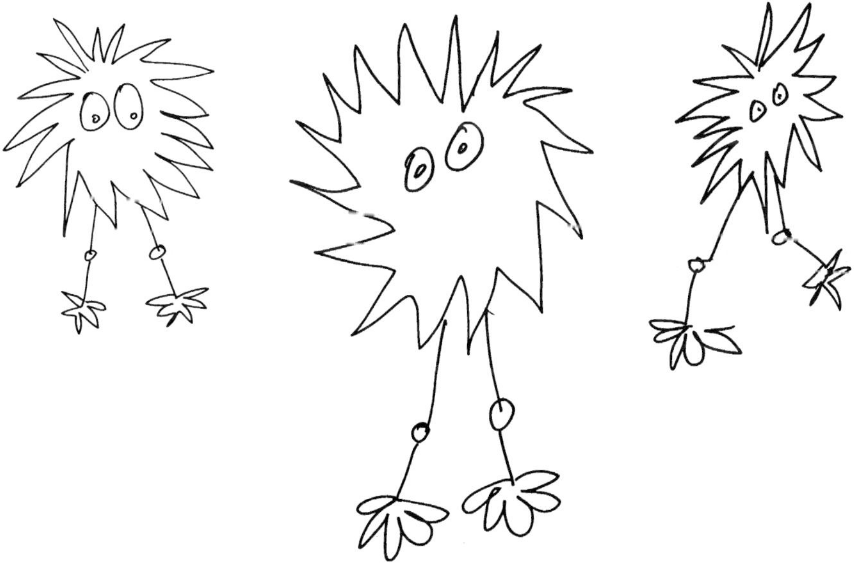

GLOOPS HAVE BIG EYES
BUT DO NOT SPEAK.

GLOOPS ARE OBSERVERS
OF EVERYTHING.

AND THEY MAKE KNOWN
THESE OBSERVATIONS.

IN THIS BOOK WE HAVE DOCUMENTED MANY OF THEIR OBSERVATIONS.

You ask "how can they communicate their observations?" Well, they write them down in their poop. You must be an expert in Glooppoopology.

GLOOPS LIKE TO WRITE ON A CLEAN SLATE. THAT IS WHY "YOU WILL SEE "DUST ME" ON A TABLE OR "WASH ME" ON THE BACK OF A TRUCK. AND NOW YOU KNOW WHERE THOSE PROFOUND WORDS COME FROM!

GLOOPISMS

# #1

WHEN YOU CHANGE
DIRECTIONS YOU
WILL END UP IN A
DIFFERENT PLACE.

# #2

THINKING DOES NOT GET YOU ANYWHERE UNLESS YOU ACT ON YOUR THINKING.

# #3

EVERYDAY A PERSON
CHANGES, THEREFORE,
EVERYDAY IS DIFFERENT.

# #4
# WHAT HAPPENS TODAY,
# NEVER HAPPENS AGAIN.

# #5

WRITING SOMETHING DOWN AND GETTING IT PUBLISHED ARE TWO DIFFERENT THINGS.

# #6

THE BEST THING
ABOUT THINGS, IS
THAT THEY EXIST.

# #7
# SADNESS MAKES
# BEING HAPPY BETTER.

# #8

IF THERE WERE NO
SHOELACES, YOU WOULD
NOT TRIP ON THEM.

#9

HAVING A HEARING AID
DOES NOT NECESSARILY
MEAN YOU HAVE TO LISTEN.

# #10
# HAVING PERFECT HEARING DOESN'T MEAN YOU ARE LISTENING.

# #11
## SOMETHING SIMPLE
## IS NOT NECESSARILY
## SIMPLE TO DO.

# #12
# A BOAT IN THE WATER NEVER STOPS MOVING.

# #14
# LISTENING IS HARDER THAN TALKING.

# #15
## A CLOSED DOOR
## HAS HINGES.

# #16
# A BOOK IS MADE
# TO BE OPENED.

# #17
TRAVELING THE STRAIGHT
AND NARROW GETS YOU
THERE QUICKER.

# #18

IF YOU CLEAN YOUR
GLASSES, YOU WILL
SEE BETTER.

# #19

WALKING UP STAIRS WILL
GET YOU TO HIGH PLACES.
WALKING DOWN IS EASIER.

# #20
## WHEN WORKING,
## SWEAT TELLS YOU THAT
## YOU HAVE DONE SOMETHING.

# #21

EDISON SAID:
10% INSPIRATION
90% PERSPIRATION

GLOOPS SAY:
10% INSPIRATION
40% CONTEMPLATION
50% PERSPIRATION
GETS THINGS
DONE EASIER.

# #22
## TO DO SOMETHING, YOU MUST START.

# #23
## TO END SOMETHING, YOU MUST FINISH.

#24
SHARING AN IDEA
CAN BE EASY, BUT
UNDERSTANDING ONE CAN
BE VERY DIFFICULT.

# #25
## Simple words make understanding easier.

# #26
## PERFECTION DOESN'T
## COME WITHOUT FAULTS.

# #27
# GETTING WET IS QUICK. DRYING TAKES TIME.

# #28
LIFE HAS A BEGINNING,
MIDDLE AND AN END.
ETERNITY IS FOREVER.

# #29
## A BIG SPLASH
## CAN RUIN ANYTHING.

# #30
## HAVING A FILTER DOESN'T MEAN THINGS WON'T GET DUSTY.

# #31
# SILENCE IS GOLD.
# NOISE IS PLUTONIUM.

# #32
## TALENT IS A GIFT. USING IT RIGHT IS A MIRACLE.

# #33
TURNING ON THE LIGHT
DOESN'T MEAN YOU'RE
NOT STILL IN THE DARK.

# #34
A TRUTH IS A TRUTH,
A LIE IS A LIE. IT'S
ALL ABOUT INTERPRETATION.

# #35
EVERYBODY CALLS SOME
THINGS DIFFERENTLY.
THAT'S WHY A CEILING
CAN BE A FLOOR.

# #36
# THE STERN
# CHANGES DIRECTION.

# #37

TREES TURN GREEN
IN THE SPRING. IF THEY
DON'T, THEY'RE DEAD.

#38
A ROCK STAYS
IN ONE PLACE,
UNLESS YOU MOVE IT.

# #39
# POTHOLES NEVER
# GO AWAY.*

*IN MICHIGAN

#40
BIRDS FLY BY DESIGN.
WE FLY ON FAITH.

# #41

WHEN THE SUN COMES
UP, THERE'S LIGHT.
WHEN THE SUN GOES DOWN,
YOU'RE IN THE DARK.

# #42
## EATING IS A NECESSITY.
## GETTING FAT ISN'T.

# #43

A ROAD MAP PROVIDES YOU MANY DIFFERENT WAYS TO GET TO YOUR DESTINATION. BUT YOU HAVE TO FOLLOW ONE IN ORDER TO GET THERE.

# #44

FAME IS WHEN
A LOT OF PEOPLE KNOW
you. BUT DO THEY?

# #45
## GREATNESS IS
## WHEN EVERYONE
## KNOWS YOU'RE GOOD.

# #46

YOU HAVE TO CLEANSE
THE DISH IN ORDER
TO GET IT CLEAN.

# #47

WINDOWS ARE TO SEE
OUT OF. WHY DO WE
PUT BLINDS ON THEM?

# #48
# CUTTING THE GRASS IS NOT THE SAME AS MOWING THE LAWN.

# #49

WHAT GOES UP ISN'T
THE PROBLEM. COMING
DOWN AND NOT BREAKING
ANYTHING IS THE TRICK.

# #50
## WHO ARE ARCHITECTS?
## IN THE PAST ARCHITECTURE
## WAS ABOUT BUILDINGS.

# #51
## NATURE IS EVERYWHERE. MAN HAS DIVIDED IT UP INTO SMALL PIECES.

# #52
# GOD IS GOD.
# THE ISMs ARE JUST
# CONFUSING.

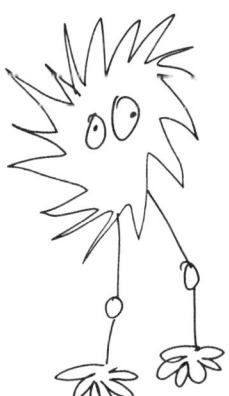

# #53
## You can change direction in a sphere but not in a circle.

# #54
## THINGS ARE THINGS
## WHATEVER THEY ARE.

# #55
## SIGNS ARE INFORMATIONAL, NOT SPIRITUAL.

# #56
# DIRT IS WHAT
# WE BUILD ON.

# #57
## WEEDS ARE JUST MISUNDERSTOOD.

# #58

AN ARCHEOLOGIST IS
ABOUT THE PAST. A TRASH
DUMP IS THEIR FUTURE.

# #59
## AN ANTIQUE IS SOMETHING OLD THAT SOMEONE WANTS.

# #60

A DIAMOND IS A LUMP
OF COAL WITH EVERYTHING
SQUEEZED OUT OF IT.

# #61
## You can see
## through a hole. What
## you see can change.

# #62
BEING CREATIVE IS EASY.
CREATING IS DIFFICULT.

# #63
# THERE IS MORE TO A POND THAN WATER.

# #64
## No turn on red.
## Except on green arrow!

# #65
# PREPARING FOR TRAVEL DOESN'T ALWAYS MAKE THE JOURNEY EXCITING!!

# #66
## FREEWAYS ARE
## REALLY EXPENSIVE.

# #67
PAYING THE PIPER
MAY ONLY MEAN YOU
BOUGHT THE NEXT DANCE.

# #68
# IF YOU DON'T LIKE SOMETHING, A LAW CAN SCREW IT UP.

# #69
## THERE ARE TWO SIDES TO A STORY. YOU HAVE TO START FROM SOMETHING.

# #70
# LOGIC IS UNBELIEVABLE.

# #71
## EVERYTHING SMELLS.

# #72

"U" MAY LOOK AT THINGS
IN A PARTICULAR WAY.
EVERYONE ELSE MAY LOOK
AT THINGS DIFFERENTLY.

# #73
# ANYTHING CAN BE DONE.
# ARE YOU FINISHED?

# #74
## SPEAKING CAN BE
## HISTORY IN THE MAKING.

# #75
# BLINDS HAVE EYES.

# #76
## BOY WAS THAT STUPID.

#77
WHAT'S "RIGHT",
TODAY, IS "LEFT"
TO TOMORROW.

# #78
# FENCES ARE GREAT
# PAPER FILTERS.

# #79
## STUPIDITY IS
## SELF-GRATIFYING.

# #80
# DOCTORS ARE WHY
# WE HAVE LAWYERS.

# #81
## A PAGE HAS TWO SIDES.

# #82
WHEN TRYING TO
FIND SOMETHING,
YOU WILL LOOK AT IT
AND NOT SEE IT.

# #83
## NOTHING IS EVER LOST.

# #84
## YOU CAN STOP A KETTLE FROM BOILING BY TURNING OFF THE HEAT.

# #85
# Hot water cools down.

# #86
## BUTTS MUST NOT
## BE LITTER BECAUSE
## THERE EVERYWHERE.

# #87
A TREE GROWS; YOU
JUST CAN'T TELL ITS
AGE UNTIL ITS DEAD.

# #88
# WINNING, A LOTTERY
# DOESN'T HAPPEN
# TO EVERYONE.

# #89
## SQUIRREL'S EAT AT BIRD FEEDERS.

# #90
## BEARS EAT WHATEVER THEY WANT.

# #91

THE END OF THE DAY
IS WHEN YOU START
SOMETHING DIFFERENT.

# #92
# THE TOP OF THE MORNING
IS THE BEGINNING
OF THE AFTERNOON,

# #93

A COMPUTER IS NOT
A LEGAL DOCUMENT.

#94

A LIBRARY IS
A COMPUTER THAT YOU
CAN SIT INSIDE.

# #95
# A COMPUTER
# GETS COBWEBS.

# #96
# A PRINTOUT IS THE
# BACKUP FOR THE INTERNET.

# #97
## COMPUTERS ARE NOT
## SAVING THE RAIN FOREST.

# #98
## A DROP CAN
## LEAVE A MARK.

# #99
# PROCRASTINATORS
# ARE TIME SAVERS.

# #100

I FIRST BECAME AWARE
OF GLOOPS IN 1964,
WHEN I WAS SERVING
ABOARD THE AIRCRAFT
CARRIER USS FRANKLIN
D. ROOSEVELT CVA42.
GLOOPS STARTED TO LEAVE
ME THEIR OBSERVATIONS
ABOUT LIFE ABOARD THAT
IMMENSE SHIP. WE PUBLISHED
THESE OBSERVATIONS
IN OUR MORNING NEWS
SHEET WHILE WE WERE
OUT TO SEA.

THERE WERE MANY OTHER STRANGE BEASTS ABOARD THE SHIP SUCH AS WAPPBATS, GREMLINS, SEABATS, JARHEADS, SWAP JOCKEYS, GRIFFINS AND BOOTS ALONG WITH NORMAL MERMAIDS AND SEA MONSTERS. NOTHING REALLY OUT OF THE ORDINARY WHILE BEING OUT TO SEA.

# GLOOPS

HAVE THEIR OWN
OPINIONS AND DO
NOT REFLECT THE VIEWS
OF THE MANAGEMENT OR
ANY OTHER GROUP THAT
WOULD CLAIM THEY KNOW
SOMETHING ABOUT THINGS.